I0785965

The Power of Friendship

Compiled by
Tenita C. Johnson

Published by So It Is Written, LLC
Detroit, MI
SoItIsWritten.net

The Power of Friendship: An Anthology
Copyright © 2023 by Tenita C. Johnson

Edited by: So It Is Written – www.SoItIsWritten.net

Formatting: Ya Ya Ya Creative – YaYaYaCreative@gmail.com

ISBN: 979-8-9888204-1-3

LCCN: 2023917464

PRINTED AND BOUND IN THE UNITED STATES OF AMERICA

Table of Contents

Visionary Author Statement

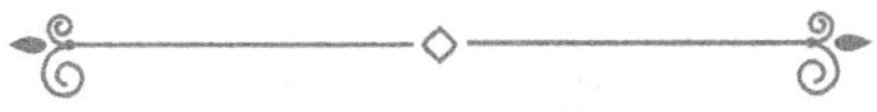

Tenita C. Johnson

For more than eight weeks, students across the Pontiac, Michigan region and surrounding areas worked to study the art of creative writing. During our time together, the students not only engaged in creative writing prompts weekly, and writing sprints, but they also had the chance to collaborate to compile this project. The students had to choose the theme of the book in which they wanted to publish as a group project and, as you can see, they agreed to write about the power of friendship.

In addition to choosing the topic, students were given the task of writing their 1,500-word story by a strict deadline. They also had to read their stories several times aloud in class weekly for feedback from their peers. In addition, the students learned how to self-edit and edit others' work. They did not edit just based on spelling, grammar and punctuation; they also had to edit the stories for consistency, tone, voice, creativity and storyline. Finally, the students worked together to choose a cover image that they all loved for the final front cover.

What you see here today is a product of weeks of hard work, dedication and consistency from students in the fifth through ninth grade who had a passion to complete a pivotal project in such a short time. Some are fictional, while others are based on their own life experiences. While many students started the class, these are the students who were dedicated to getting to the finish line. I want to personally thank The City of Pontiac and the students' parents for showing up for these students weekly for the program.

The stories you are about to read are a full reflection of their creativity and artistic genius. Enjoy as these students take you into their worlds of experiencing the power of friendship!

Tenita "Bestseller" Johnson

About the Visionary Author

Transforming pain into purpose is a gift that authorpreneur, speaker and book coach, Tenita "Bestseller" Johnson gives to everyone she encounters. She is a warrior of words with a fierce passion for guiding authors to expand their brand by showing them how to earn multiple streams of income from just ONE book. As the author of eighteen books, seven of which have been Amazon bestsellers, she is living proof that sharing your story leads to your destiny.

Familiar with rising from numerous fires and coming out unscathed, Tenita has triumphed over suicidal thoughts, depression, low self-esteem, marital storms and blended family woes. She has also endured miscarriages and the still birth of twins the day after she married her husband. Each of these tragedies has added indelible layers to her resilience. With more than 25 years in journalism, writing and editing, she has a knack for creating narratives that are authentic and raw, yet endearingly relatable. She is a vessel with the ability to change lives and impact the world, thus she is a proud "book bully," who relentlessly urges others to, "Write the book and get paid for the pain!"

When Tenita speaks, people listen with their ears as well as their hearts and souls because her transparency transcends pretense. She is a bold beacon of hope who inspires others to seek their highest peak. One of her proudest and defining moments was her appearance on Kirk Franklin's Praise Sirius XM channel.

As the founder and CEO of So It Is Written Publishing, she has helped hundreds of authors birth their books in record time. The 12-year-old company excels as a one stop shop for the complete book process from conception to completion, not just editing. The editorial guru successfully helps people to pen books that will boost their brand, accelerate their paydays and bust open doors of endless opportunities. So It Is Written won The Sunrise Pinnacle Award for Diversity Company of the Year, in 2020, from the Rochester Regional Chamber of Commerce in Rochester, Michigan. For six years, Tenita hosted the Red Ink Conference in Atlanta, Detroit, Charlotte and Chicago. Over 600 attendees received invaluable information from industry leaders on how to write, edit, market and publish their next bestseller.

Beyond her books, her versatility shines in multiple areas, including her role as the executive producer of the hit stage play, *When the Smoke Clears*, which was based on her book, *When the Smoke Clears: A Phoenix Rises*. The play ran in 2017 and 2018 to sold-out audiences in downtown Detroit. She also served as the editorial director for *Career Mastered Magazine* and *Hope for Women Magazine* for years.

Tenita's passion for delivering bestselling books is matched only by her devotion to helping women and men heal from the drama, trauma and baggage of sexual abuse. Her 2021 anthology, *HUSH: Breaking the Cycle of Silence Around Sexual Abuse*, features eight women who lost their innocence and identity to life-altering trauma, followed by *HUSH II*, which highlighted both men and women who have survived sexual abuse. She is a huge advocate and mouthpiece for those who have been sexually abused as she empowers them to release their pain instead of suffering in silence.

Her future plans include the release of *HUSH III*, producing her short film *What Happens in This House*, and completing the script for her feature film *When the Smoke Clears*. As a catalyst for positive change, she is a woman who has learned to live an intentional life of purpose while unapologetically fulfilling her God-driven assignments.

For booking or speaking engagements, email info@soitiswritten.net or visit www.tenitajohnson.com.

Cultivating Courage through Friendship

Jakenzy Geter

She shoots and scores! The Las Vegas Aces win the championship!

Hi! I'm Ma'kayla. Let me tell you how the power of friendship helped get me to the WNBA. I was on summer break. The next school year, I was going to be a freshman in high school. One day, I was sitting at home, watching the WNBA on TV. I enjoyed watching it. I started thinking about what I wanted to do for my future, and basketball was top of mind. I wanted to see if I was any good at it. So, I grabbed my dad's basketball and walked down to the park.

When I got to the park, I started stretching. After I shot the ball, I made it on my first try. I was so happy.

Wow! This really brings me joy! I thought to myself. I continued shooting and making baskets. I even made a few half courts. Two hours went by, and I decided to walk back home. When I got home, I saw my dad. I was excited to tell him about how much I loved basketball and how much I wanted to play. I had a big smile on my face while I told my dad about what happened. I didn't expect what happened next.

He took the ball from me and said, "I don't like the idea of you playing basketball. I don't feel like females should play basketball, even though there are some female basketball players in the WNBA. They are really talented. That's how they get to play in the WNBA. Plus, where is this new interest in playing basketball coming from? There's only a slight chance that you can make it into the WNBA. You'd be better off being a doctor."

As he said that, the smile on my face slowly faded. I looked at him and said, "Okay."

I ran in the house and called my best friend Saniyya. We'd been best friends since kindergarten. She has always been there for me.

"Don't cry," she said. "I believe you can make it if you put in enough hard work. Don't let anyone tell you that you can't or shouldn't play if that's what you really want to do."

I wiped my tears and told her, "Thank you. I really needed that."

We talked for a while before getting off the phone. I took a shower and went to sleep. The next morning, I heard someone knocking on my bedroom door. I was confused.

Who could that be? I thought. I walked to my door and opened it. It was Saniyya. I was happy to see her, but I was confused at how she got into my house.

Before I asked, she said, "Your dad let me in. Get dressed. We're going to the park to practice playing basketball!"

I smiled and got dressed. I dribbled the ball until we got to the park. Saniyya helped me practice. We went to the park every day and practiced, in fact. When school started, I studied really hard and got straight A's. I was happy when basketball season came. I didn't know if I should try out for the team or not. I asked Saniyya, and she confirmed that I should try out. I went home and asked my dad if I could try out for the team. He looked like he didn't want me to, but he said, "Yes."

I was so happy! I ran to my room and called Saniyya to tell her the good news. She was happy for me, too. The next day, I went to tryouts and Saniyya was there with me. I made the team, and I was so happy. I went to breakfast every day and, every day, Saniyya came with me. When I went to my first game, I was so excited. I looked in the crowd to see if my dad was there. I searched everywhere, but I didn't see him. I saw Saniyya in the crowd though, so that made me happy.

When halftime came, we were in the lead 43-36. We won the game, and I was so excited. The team and I went out to eat to celebrate. I went home and told my dad that we had won the game and knew he'd be just as excited as I was.

He said, "That's good, but that's only high school basketball. That's nothing compared to the WNBA."

I didn't say anything. I simply shook my head and went upstairs. I took a shower, made me some food, and went to sleep. When I woke up, I called Saniyya to tell her how my dad responded to the great news.

"Remember what I said," she said. "You did good. I'm proud of you, girl."

I smiled and told her, "Meet me at the park so we can practice."

We practiced for about five hours before we went to get something to eat.

A few years later, I was at a WNBA game with Saniyya. We had VIP passes. It was so much fun. We were out of town, so we had to stay at a hotel. When we were getting a room, we ran into Candace Parker.

"Oh my gosh! It's Candace!" I screamed.

"Who's Candace?" Saniyya asked.

"Only one of the world's best WNBA players!"

I walked over to her. "Can I please get a picture with you?" I asked Candace.

"Of course!" she said. After we took the picture, I told her about my dream to be in the WNBA.

"I believe in you," she said. "Just keep putting in hard work, and you'll succeed," she said. I gave her a hug and thanked her for the picture and the words of wisdom. When Saniyya and I got back to our hometown, I told my dad. He didn't believe that I'd met Candace until I showed him the picture.

"Well, that still doesn't mean you'll make it," he said. "You haven't even got a scholarship to play for a college basketball team. You only have one more game left. Plus, this is the last game of the season and it's your last year of school before college. So, you might as well start making a backup plan."

"Why don't you believe I can do it?" I blurted out. "Why don't you support me? I've been trying really hard, and you don't care! I've been playing basketball since ninth grade, and you haven't shown up to any of my games. Maybe if you were there that would encourage me and help me. I've won every game. I haven't lost one. I'm the best on my team. The recruits are coming to visit for the last game. So, it would be nice if you could at least come to this game."

My dad stood there in shock. I ran to my room before he could say anything. I went to sleep sad that night. When my last game came up, I had to really focus on winning because the recruits were there. I gave Saniyya a big hug before I played. When I walked out onto the court, I saw my dad in the crowd, and I smiled. At halftime, it was tied 56 to 56. I was tired, but I had to push through.

The other team was in the lead by two points and there were only five seconds left in the game. I was on the half-court line when my teammate passed me the ball. I shot it and I made a three-pointer! The buzzer went off, and me and my team cheered because we had won. It was because of the shot I'd made!

As we celebrated, a recruiter came up to me from Stanford University. They wanted me to play basketball for them. Of course, I agreed! I was so happy that I had gotten into a college to play basketball. My dad was shocked, as well.

"Well, you made it to college basketball, but still not the WNBA," he said.

Suddenly, all of my joy went away. I was sad that I had made remarkable success, yet he still wasn't proud of me. A few months later, I was getting ready for my first game. I was excited, but I was also sad because Saniyya couldn't make it to the game. I knew she was there with me in spirit. Even though I'd played in college, I had to sign up for the WNBA draft. I'll never forget the day I heard the announcement.

"Ma'kayla Smith has been drafted to the Las Vegas Aces!"

I was so happy that I'd made it to the WNBA. I called my dad to tell him the good news. For the first time in my life, my dad told me he was proud of me.

"I didn't think you could make it, but you did," he said. "I'm proud of you, Ma'kayla."

"Thanks, dad," I replied.

I called Saniyya to tell her the good news.

"I knew you could do it, friend! I'm proud of you!"

But if it wasn't for Saniyya's help, I would've never had enough confidence to even try out for the basketball team. I wouldn't have had enough courage to play. Thanks to her help and friendship, I was able to make it to the WNBA.

POSITIVE FRIENDSHIP THOUGHTS

Friendship to the Rescue

Jabari Potts

Once upon a time, there were two boys named Jeremy and John. They were best friends. They liked folding paper. Jeremy liked making all types of origami, and John liked specifically making paper airplanes. They liked showing each other their newest creations, but sometimes they would argue about whose model was the best.

One day, they got into a huge argument because John had ripped up Jeremy's new creation. Jeremy told John that he did not want to be friends with him, and John agreed. So, they both went their separate ways. John felt bad for ripping up Jeremy's model, but Jeremy did not want to forgive John. The next day, Jeremy was out walking when two men in military-like suits demanded money. However, he didn't have any money on him. So, he instead gave the men an origami model he had stashed in his pocket. Since the model was so cool, the two men accepted it and they decided to take Jeremy, too. John tried to call Jeremy to apologize, but he didn't answer his phone. John went to

Jeremy's house. But, to his surprise, he saw guards at Jeremy's house. Then he saw a man in a black uniform leaving Jeremy's house.

John followed him into his van, and he saw Jeremy lying on his back.

John told him, "I came to the house to apologize."

He saw the guards and figured something else was up. The van started moving. John and Jeremy tried to find a way out, but it was impossible. After several hours, the van stopped, and the two guards took John and Jeremy out. The guards took them inside of a massive building and put them into a holding cell.

John quietly told Jeremy, "This can't be a government facility because our Miranda Rights were violated."

Jeremy asked, "Who is Miranda?"

There were two beds, a toilet, and a sink inside the room that the guards put them in. As soon as the guards left, John and Jeremy began bickering.

"It's all your fault we've been kidnapped!" John claimed. "You shouldn't have been naïve enough to go walking out at night!"

Jeremy responded, "No, this is all your fault! I wouldn't even be here. If we were still friends, I would have been hanging out with you!"

In the end, Jeremy and John decided to set aside their differences and work together to escape.

Jeremy told John, "I never leave the house without extra origami folding paper."

John caught on immediately. John fashioned a key out of the paper and put the key into the keyhole. To their surprise, the key unlocked the door. They both were so happy. John opened the door, and they slipped out. Then they found an old telephone booth with clothes. They disguised themselves as one of the henchmen with the clothes and walked out of the telephone booth. One of the guards noticed that the two boys went missing and notified all of the other guards of their disappearance. The guards then put the place on lockdown.

Soon, however, the two boys' disguises started to wear off.

John told Jeremy, "We should find a place to hide."

They thought they were in the clear until one of the guards noticed the two boys. The guard that noticed them sent out an alert to the rest of the guards. Then, John and Jeremy made a mad dash. John noticed a big piece of paper, and he didn't hesitate to point it out to Jeremy. John made a big paper airplane. To their surprise, the paper airplane was made out of a special crafting material that made the paper airplane able to hold its weight. Jeremy attached some propellers, and they started flying at the guards outside the room. The guards scattered and ran as their formations were broken by the path of the paper airplane. One of the guards threw his staff at the paper airplane, causing it to veer off course. Jeremy and John had to jump out of the plane to escape the crash. All of the guards formed a circle around John and Jeremy. Recognizing defeat, the boys allowed themselves to be led back to their holding cell.

Jeremy wondered aloud if they were ever going to make it out of there alive. John reassured Jeremy, "Eventually, we are bound to find a way out."

Jeremy grabbed a piece of metallic paper that he had hidden in his pocket and proceeded to create an origami Swiss army knife so they could cut their way through the bars of the cell. After Jeremy finished cutting the cell bars off, they looked both ways before exiting their cell. They had to find a place to hide and plan their escape. After running for a few minutes, they found a slightly open door and they went in. There was a guard inside. They quickly silenced the guard so he wouldn't alert the other guards in the area. Jeremy quickly explained the situation to the guard, and the guard let John take his uniform. John would then pretend to take Jeremy back to his cell.

After walking for a while, they approached an elevator and tried to figure out how to operate it. John checked the uniform that he had borrowed from the guard and found that it contained a key card that made the red light above the elevator turn green. They went down to the next floor, and there were several guards down there, waiting for the elevator to arrive. They exited the elevator untouched and proceeded down a corridor. They entered a room that was dimly lit. It turned out to be a supply closet. They found the same uniform that the guards around the base were wearing and got everything they needed to disguise Jeremy. They left the room and proceeded along the corridor in the direction from which they came.

A guard walked up to them and asked, "Do you know where the prisoners are?"

They both assured the guard that they knew nothing about the prisoners or where they were. Hardly believing their luck, they proceeded along the hallway. The two boys weren't accustomed to the heavy military-like uniforms that the guards were wearing. Soon, they struggled to breathe with the masks over their faces. They decided to take a break, figuring that it was unlikely that a guard would notice their faces. What they didn't know was that along with an alert of the escaped prisoners, pictures of their faces were released. They came to realize that when a guard turned the corner. They looked shocked for a second, then they ran. Nobody is a match for a person who is running for fear of their life. Jeremy and John took off at top speed and quickly outdistanced the guard that was pursuing them. They both turned left and found the nearest emergency signal that was mounted onto the wall. Without wasting a second, Jeremy fumbled around for the key card that he placed in one of his pockets. He swiped the card and deactivated the alarm. The two boys high-fived each other because there was no doubt that Jeremy's quick thinking saved them some valuable time.

Working quickly, John pulled some paper out of his pocket and shaped it into a throwing knife. He stabbed tiny holes into it so it would make a loud whistling noise while it was in flight. He threw it down the hallway. When no guards appeared to see what it was that was making that noise, they proceeded in the direction in which they threw it. They found a staircase with an exit sign in front of the door and proceeded as fast as they could down the stairs. There must have been a motion sensor somewhere on the stairs because an alarm blared loudly suddenly, and guards poured out onto the stairs. They reached the bottom and exited the building.

The building looked massive from the outside. Their marvel at the size of the building was cut short by the number of guards pursuing them and the geographic feature of the perimeter surrounding the building. Water was surrounding the building, almost similar to a moat in a medieval castle. Without hesitation, the two boys took off their guard uniforms and made their way into the water. John decided that taking off his vest was a lost cause and he proceeded into the water. The boys didn't know what hit them. The current was strong enough to sweep them from a standing position and pulled them deeper into the waves. Jeremy was struggling to stay afloat, but John managed to keep his head above water. Suddenly, they saw a boat coming toward them. John latched onto Jeremy and managed to keep both of them afloat. John realized that there was a built-in flotation device in the vest that he had borrowed from the guards. The boys could have died from relief as the lights on top of the boats flashed red, white and blue. They knew that the police were there to save them.

Once they reached the boat, the police threw them life preservers and reeled them into the boat. Safely on land, they told the story of being kidnapped and taken to the base of the unknown secret organization. Looking back on it, neither boy was completely sure why they'd been arguing in the first place.

After all, if it wasn't for their friendship, they wouldn't have made it out of the building alive.

POSITIVE FRIENDSHIP THOUGHTS

The Power of Friendship

Chloe Martin

Amelia was attending her first day of second grade. She was extremely nervous and extremely excited. She nervously walked into the school and saw a bunch of kids talking. As they all closed their lockers, they went to their classrooms. She saw the principal, who was approaching her with a warm smile on her face.

"Hello!" the principal said. "Welcome to the Royalty of Bears School! I am your new principal, Principal Martinez! Your class is down the hall. Would you like me to walk with you to your class?"

Amelia stood there silently. After a couple of seconds, she finally murmured, "Yes."

They walked down the hall until they reached the classroom. Amelia's heart was beating faster than ever as the principal unlocked the door and walked into the classroom. All of the kids were talking about who the new student could be.

The principal said, "Silence everyone! I have a big announcement!"

All the kids stopped talking.

"As you know, we have a new student who has decided to join our school! Please give a warm welcome to Amelia!"

The principal held her hand out to Amelia as Amelia entered the classroom and made a nervous smile.

I hope I don't look weird, Amelia said in her mind.

Then one boy started laughing at her before he said, "You look like a donkey!"

Everyone laughed with him, except one girl.

The girl said, "Hey! Stop that! That's very rude!"

"Yes, Olivia. I agree with you. Very rude, Samuel. Go to my office immediately!" the principal said.

"Yes, Ms. Martinez," the boy said sadly. When the boy and Ms. Martinez walked out, Olivia walked up to Amelia.

"Don't worry about him. He bullies new people all the time, and he always goes to the principal's office. When he does, he fakes being sad."

"Oh, that's sad to hear," Amelia said.

"Hey, by the way … do you wanna be friends?" Olivia asked.

"Sure!" Amelia said.

From that day on, Amelia and Olivia were by each other's side. When they got hurt, they helped each other get back up. When they got bullied, they stood up for each other. One day, there was a tough boy in school who always liked to pick on the second graders. He was in the fifth grade. He always got on everybody's nerves. Many people called him Tough Bully.

As Amelia was going to her locker to get her snack, the fifth grader walked up to her and said, "Hey, weirdo!"

"What do you want, Boyce?" Amelia asked in an annoyed tone.

"I want you to do my homework since you're so smart," Boyce said while smirking.

"And why exactly are you asking a second grader to do it when there are plenty of fifth graders who know how to do the homework?" Amelia said with a questionable face.

"Because they're dumb, and they aren't as smart as you are."

He grabbed Amelia and was about to take her to the library, until Olivia stepped in.

Olivia said, "Hey! Leave Amelia alone, you banana!"

"And what are you gonna do about it? I'm one of the toughest boys in the whole school. Nobody can stop me. Besides, you're too weak. It will only take me five…"

Just then, Amelia kicked Boyce in the stomach and smacked him hard in the face.

"Owww!" Boyce said while screaming in pain.

Both girls high fived each other and ran down to the hallway to go tell the principal about how Boyce had bullied them.

"Boyce, I'm very shocked at your horrifying behavior! You will be suspended for two weeks. There is no bullying allowed in this school. Do you understand me?" the principal asked in a stern voice.

"Yes, Ms. Martinez," he said in a low, sad tone.

"Well then. Don't just stand there. Pack everything and leave the school immediately!" Boyce walked away, shedding more tears.

"Thank you, girls, for telling me about this horrific act. That is extremely unacceptable in this school. If he ever does it again, please inform me. Understand?"

"Understood!" the girls said.

The girl skipped down the hallway, knowing that the annoying boy was gone, and they wouldn't have any more trouble for two weeks at least. Amelia invited Olivia to her house for a sleepover. They both talked about Boyce and how they were extremely annoyed by him. Then, they took some time to play games, watch a movie, eat popcorn and get some rest. In the morning, they were refreshed and ready for another day. They had more bullies come after them over the years, but they always stuck together. They fought them off together. They always did everything together, and they always told each other their biggest secrets. They even shared their lunch! They grew old together and remained best friends for many years.

The power of friendship comes with different advantages. You have a person to talk to about everything and you also do many things together. Friendship is priceless and powerful beyond measure.

POSITIVE FRIENDSHIP THOUGHTS

The Amazing Rescue

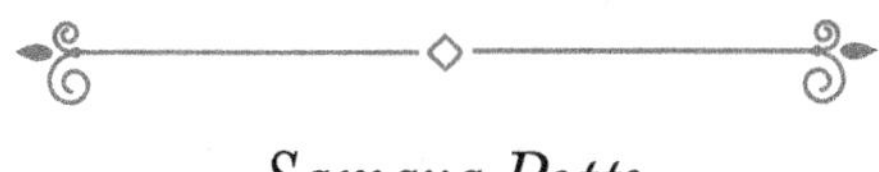

Samaya Potts

The scientist's disappointment was inconsequential as all subjects had conveniently escaped. They were facing arrest for conducting harmful tests, but Samaya had already called the police, and the case went dark. Wiggy sensed the danger, and it was clear they had to leave instantly, but not independently.

"Get up, Viggy! We're departing now," Wiggy affirmed as she woke her twin.

"I'm up. Where are we proceeding? It's 1 a.m. How many belongings should I bring?" Viggy asked as she packed.

After crowding the car, Viggy proposed bringing the other twins, too. But Wiggy was already ahead of her. They gathered up the other twins, and Viggy put the car on auto mode, authorizing her to rest. After three days of driving, they reached Viggy's cabin, close to the lab, but not too close to bypass getting caught. They unpacked their belongings. They went to sleep.

In the morning, they had pancakes, eggs, sausage and grits. When they went out of the house, they snuck into the building lab and Sunlight overheard, "You little brat!"

A scientist said, "Never!"

Samaya said, "Your new name is Phoenix."

"You are a mess up and will never be fixed," the scientist said.

Phoenix got so mad that she turned into a dragon and killed the scientist. When she turned back into a human, she had a dragon tail and horns. She also had markings of a queen on her cheeks.

"How you like that for a brat?" she said with confidence.

When they were inside the lab, they heard a scream that sounded more like a laugh. It sounded like Phoenix's laugh.

"Let's go inside to see what's going on," Sunlight said.

"You think we should? It sounds a bit threatening in there. Plus, did you not listen to all of the screaming … I mean, giggling?" Wiggy said.

"I know that laugh from anywhere. It's Phoenix's," Moonlight said with satisfaction in her eyes. Nearly roaring, Sunlight broke the door open and let out the biggest, fattest riot of joy she conceivably could do. She practically lost her voice because she was so happy to see her companion alive.

"Be quiet, you idiot! Are you trying to get us caught?" Viggy asked, smacking her on the back of the head.

"Ouch! That hurt."

"I'm sorry. I'm just so excited," Moonlight said.

"Let's get in and get out. We have no time to waste. No one knows we're here," Sunlight said.

"Go! Go! Go! We heard someone. Someone broke into the building. Put the whole building on lockdown now. We cannot lose whoever is in the building. I repeat, put the building on lockdown! Put the building on lockdown," the scientist said on the PA system.

"Shoot! Thanks a lot. You got us caught. Now we have to hide before it's too late," Wiggy said, running.

They hid in an oversized cabinet that was sufficiently fit for all four of them. Three guards trekked right past them. As they were climbing out of the box, they heard a big boom. Soon enough, there were guards in front of them, behind them and on both sides of them. They attempted not to roar. Then, Sunlight noticed there was a big void through which they could skate. So, they got through and started running to the exit. They made it out just in time. They ran to the private house, where no one could see it— not even the guard. As the guards lost sight of them, they turned back around and went into the lab.

"That was such a close one! We could have gotten caught. Luckily, we didn't. I put a tracker on one of the guards. It's a camera that's so small that not even the human eye could see it. We'd have to use a microscope. I can see where the guard is going. It's an easy way to get in and not get caught," Viggy said.

They went inside and went to bed. The next day, they put on their clothes, ate breakfast and snuck into the lab again. This time, they were more cautious of their surroundings. They heard pounding on the glass.

"It's early in the morning. Do you think we should be here? We could get caught again, even though you installed all those cameras. Plus, you realize that if we get caught, we might get put into one of the rooms and then get tested on again?" Sunlight said tiptoeing.

"Look! I found Phoenix. She's lying down in bed. We have to be quiet not to wake her up or, as you've noticed, she will go crazy," Moonlight said as she opened the door to her room.

"So, are you going to talk to her, or am I? If I perish, it's your fault. One of you is to blame!"

"I will do it because all of you are big, chubby scaredy cats. We all know I'm the best and bravest one here. So, let the pro into the room. I'll do it under one condition: one of you has to come in with me," Sunlight said.

"Bet! I'll go with you. But if she wakes up, we both run or hide," Wiggy said. They waved good luck to the two and went into hiding. As soon as they went into the room, Phoenix woke up. To her surprise, her friends were there to help her.

"Hi, guys! So, are you all going to get me out of here so we can go back home, and I can leave this place? I can probably live with you if you're okay with that. After that, we can go live our happily ever after hopefully very joyful life," she said smiling.

They weren't expecting that to happen.

"Let's go. We got to get out of here before we got caught. We already got caught once, and we don't want to get caught again. So, let's get out of here as fast as we can. We don't have time to waste," Moonlight said as she took off the shock collar from her neck.

They snuck out of the lab and went back to the private house, where nobody could find them.

"We are so glad to see you," Wiggy said happily. They all went into a really large group hug. Phoenix was crying. She told them everything that happened. Then, Moonlight had the plan to go back and collect evidence that the scientists were doing terrible things. Sunlight got a call.

"Hello. This is *********. We are searching for a girl named ****. Have you seen her anywhere? The last place someone saw her was at **********," a voice on the phone said.

"No, I have not seen a girl named ****," Sunlight said with confusion on her face. The caller hung up the phone.

"Who was that?" Phoenix asked.

"I don't know," Sunlight said.

Thunder! A loud noise hit the foundation. Moonlight darted to the foundation, and she saw a little girl that looked approximately six years old with sky blue hair and another girl who looked approximately four years old with dark blue hair.

"Hi, little fellas! What's your girl's name?" Viggy asked.

"My name is Eri, and this is my baby sister. Her name is Jade," the girl with sky blue hair said.

Sunlight heard they were looking for the younger one.

"We will let you stay with us. You and your sister can come back home with us," Wiggy said.

"First, let's get you some new clothes, even if they are a bit too big for you," Moonlight said. When they got them some clean clothes, they asked them what their powers were.

Eri said that she could create anything she wanted if she looked at a picture of it first. Jade had omnipotence, which meant she had all power. The girls said that Phoenix was their mother and she had just forgotten all about them.

The next day, they started to drive home. On the way, they ran into an old enemy. Quickly, Phoenix called the police. The police came and arrested the man. Then, the police were shown to the lab. They arrested the scientists, and the scientists were put into prison for forty years because of harmful tests on kids. When they arrived home, Phoenix, Eri and Jade took a blood test to see if they were related to each other. When the results came in, the results were 98.5% positive.

All seven girls moved into a big house together.

Jade said the scientist would be back for them, and only them. Viggy was scared that she might be right. As they were going to bed, they heard a loud noise coming from the gaming room.

"Let's go check it out," Wiggy said as she poked Moonlight in the forehead.

As they went downstairs, they saw a little dritten (dragon kitten) lying on the floor.

"Awwww! Let's keep it! Please! Please!" Wiggy said.

Sure enough, they got to keep the dritten.

They lived happily ever after ... or did they?

POSITIVE FRIENDSHIP THOUGHTS

Always Be a Good Friend

Jania Gracey

Hi! I'm Selena, and I'm a cheerleader. One day, I was sitting down, and my good friend Mari came over. She was a cheerleader, too. She always came over to my house to practice. When she came over, Mari helped me study because she was really smart. Her parents thought she was wasting her time doing cheer. They thought she should only focus on school. While we were practicing, Mari was having trouble with her routine, and she kept doubting herself.

She kept saying things like, "I should have listened to my parents and just quit!"

I tried to tell her that she was going to be fine. But she wouldn't listen.

The next day, Mari decided to come to my house after school. However, we didn't practice cheerleading. As soon as we finished studying, she went home. We had school the next day. When I got there, Mari was sitting down outside, crying. It was almost like she didn't even know I was there.

I asked her, "What's wrong?"

She didn't tell me, so I just sat there with her. When school started, she still wanted to sit there. But I had to go to class, so I left. I tried to get her to come with me, but she just sat there and cried. At lunchtime, I went looking everywhere for her. I checked the cafeteria. I checked on the playground. I checked the gym. I couldn't find her anywhere. Finally, I saw her walking in the hallway, but she was still crying. I didn't know what to do. I didn't want to make her think I was just being nosey, so I decided to give her space.

The very next day, she came over to my house after school.

"Girl, what was wrong with you yesterday" I asked.

She didn't say anything. I thought maybe she didn't hear me. So, I asked her again. But this time, I looked her right in the eyes.

"What was bothering you yesterday?"

This time, I was positive she heard me. Mari looked down, took a couple of steps back and dropped her head.

She said, "Don't worry about it. It's not important."

I tried to get her to talk to me. But the more I asked, the more upset she became. We decided to start practicing our routine because the competition was coming up. I didn't say a word about it the rest of the night. We ended up practicing a long time before Mari finally went home.

The day of the competition, we were so nervous. I was sweating and I had butterflies in my stomach. They called my cheer team's name. We went on stage. Eight counts into my routine, I fell flat on my face, and everyone laughed. Mari tried to come hug me, but my cheer coach stopped her. I struggled to get back up. But when I finally did, I ran backstage to my mom. My cheer team performed the entire routine without me, like I was never there. After the competition, we went back to the hotel. The whole team was laughing at me. Mari tried to hug me, but I didn't let her because I thought she was laughing, too. She tried to tell me she wasn't, but that did not help the fact that I was still hurt inside. I decided to go to my room and just go to bed.

The next morning, I went down for breakfast. The moment I stepped in, my stomach dropped. Mari was already there, but she was sitting with other people! *How could she do this to me?* I thought. We *always* ate together every morning. But, when I thought about it, I honestly couldn't blame her. Now that I think about it, I was super rude. I let my emotions get the best of me. I told myself that I could never let that happen. She had been my friend for four years. I decided to sit down by myself because everyone else was laughing. I wondered why they were laughing.

Then it hit me: someone probably posted on social media. I searched and, sure enough, someone had. I ran out of school and all the way back home. I was greeted by my dad, who was doing work. So, I just went to my room and locked the door.

Later, my mom came home and was wondering why my door was locked. She knocked on the door. When I opened the door, my mom and Mari were standing right there. My mom walked away.

I asked Mari, "Why are you here?"

She said, "I'm here to say sorry, but I wasn't laughing with the rest of the crowd."

I started to question myself for treating her like that. I apologized to her, and we made up. In fact, she came into my room, and we practiced. After practice, Mari helped me study for my math test the next day. The next day, I was scared. We sat down next to each other during lunch. Right after lunch was the math test.

Mari looked at me and said, "You will be fine, just like you always are. Remember what I taught you."

I took the test and got my results back. I got an A+ and Mari celebrated with me. Now, it was time to focus on the upcoming cheerleading competition. We were both nervous, so we decided to practice at my house again. We both did amazingly well! This time, she was on my team. A week later was the competition. We rode together to the competition because Mari's parents didn't always come to our competitions. We laughed a lot in the car before we made it to the hotel. We got food and went to bed, knowing we had such a long day ahead of us.

The next day was the competition. I was practically jumping out of my skin. I woke up, got in the shower and got ready. Mari and I got on the bus, and we were ready to go. Once we got there, we got our makeup and hair done. We were the first ones to go on stage, and we blew everyone away.

We waited for everyone to go, and we got ready for the awards ceremony. When award time came, we were nervous. All of the groups did so good. But when they finally announced that first place went to our team, I jumped up in shock! We got a trophy and medals. We went back to the hotel and went to bed. The next day, we went back home. I was so happy when we got back. We had a cheer sister sleepover with all the cheerleaders from my team. We had fun. We danced and even had a dance battle. One of the cheer moms took us to the pool, where we had so much fun. When we got back to the gym, we played Truth, Dare, Double Dare, Promise to Repeat. We were up all night.

We had practice on the next day. While we were tumbling, Mari twisted her ankle. She started crying and was rushed to the hospital. I was in the back with her, as well as her parents. Her parents kept telling her, "This is exactly why you need to stick with school and become a lawyer!"

That's when it hit me that was probably the reason she was crying that one day. I didn't say anything because her parents were right there. Once we got to the hospital, her parents kicked me out of the hospital room. I never knew her parents were so mean. The doctors told us that she had a concussion and a sprained ankle. This would definitely affect her cheering.

Her parents had the biggest, most disgusting grins on their faces.

The doctor came back in and said, "I forgot to mention that she cannot go to school for about three weeks."

It looked like her parents were about to be on fire. They stormed out of the hospital. I told Mari she could stay with my family until her parents came to their senses. She thanked me and my parents came to pick us up. She stayed with us until she got better. Her first cheer practice back, she was nervous she was going to get hurt. After we talked, she became more confident in herself, and we had a successful cheer practice.

That night, both of us realized how important our friendship really was!

POSITIVE FRIENDSHIP THOUGHTS

Neighborhood Friends

Nyla Johnson

Ever since me and Tyler met on the school bus, we've been friends. I am in the sixth grade, but Tyler is going into the fifth grade. I like to play the drums, sing and dance. I'm also in the process of learning how to play the saxophone.

On my first day of fifth grade, I was on the bus. A Black boy named Tyler got on the bus. I knew I was going to see him more often because he lived in my neighborhood. So, I told him to come sit next to me on the bus.

He asked, "Do you want to be friends?"

I said, "Yes!"

He told me more about himself. "My name is Tyler. I am ten years old. I have one baby sister and three brothers."

Over the school year, Tyler and I became best friends.

At our school, there was a path that went from our neighborhood all the way to my school. By the middle of the school year, Tyler would meet me at my house in the mornings because my house was closer to the path to school. From the meetup spot, we would ride our bikes to the school on the path. After school, since fifth grade classes got dismissed before fourth graders, I would wait outside on the bench until Tyler came out. Then, we rode our bikes on the path back home.

While we were riding home from school on Halloween, I asked, "Hey! How did you know where I lived? I never told you."

He said, "Well, I asked your friend Susie. She showed me on the bus when we passed it on the way back from school."

Then I said, "Ohhhh! Well, if you know where I live, it's only fair that I know where you live."

So, Tyler took me to his house and showed me around the outside of the house. He had two plum trees in the front yard, a blackberry and raspberry tree in the back, a cherry tree in the front, and tomato bushes in the back. He also had a trampoline.

After school and on weekends, we would first pick some plums, raspberries and blackberries. Then, we spent the rest of our time playing on the trampoline. Sometimes, we went to the cider mill with his brother Justin and our other two friends, Veronica and Breslyn. Veronica is eleven years old. She's in the same grade as me. She has blueish-grayish eyes and black hair. She has three older brothers, and she also lives in my neighborhood. Breslyn has teal eyes and blonde hair. She always wears crop tops, shorts and hoodies. She also lives in my neighborhood. She has two older brothers and a dog. I met Breslyn at school, but I know Veronica from an ice cream truck. Veronica does not go to the same school.

One day, me and Tyler rode to school on our bikes. Tyler does not like spider webs! He stopped me by the gate before we even entered the path because he saw a spider web. He asked me if I could run through it so it wouldn't get in his face. I did just that.

He said, "Thank you so much!"

"You are so welcome," I said. "But can we get to the path now? My teacher is going to kill me if I am late."

When we got onto the path, Tyler saw another spider web. But I didn't see it that time.

So, he simply said one word, "Nyla!"

I walked through the spider web and right in the middle, he said, "Watch out for the spider!"

I am deathly afraid of spiders! So, when I saw it, I screamed and threw my bike on the ground. Then, I started running around. Tyler grabbed my big, blue water bottle with stickers on it.

He said, "Here! Let me whack it off your bike. Then, we can go."

"But then it would be on my water bottle!"

He put my water bottle back and used his instead. After he knocked the spider off, he picked up my bike. He made sure there was no spider on my bike before he said, "Okay! We can go now!"

We rode up the hill to the spot where we park our bikes. When we got off the bikes, we realized that the only bus left in the bus loop was the last bus dropping off students. We were going to be late! Even though we ran toward the doors, they were locked by the time we reached them. So, we had to walk to the front of the building and sign ourselves in at the office.

We walked to our classrooms. Good thing for us, our classes were right next to each other. We said, "Goodbye!" and I waited for him at the end of the day, as normal. I was waiting outside for him when he came out and we asked each other at the same time, "Did you get in trouble for being late?"

We both said, "No!" as we laughed.

When we got on our bikes, we had to stop because we saw a vulture. Tyler actually got attacked by a vulture before, so that is why he stopped me. He was afraid. We sat quietly, waiting for it to fly away. After twenty minutes, it finally flew away. We rushed onto our bikes to get to the road as soon as possible.

We said to each other, "Today is just not our day. First, the spider webs. Then, the spider. Then being late! Today is just a bad luck day for us!"

The main takeaway for this story is to never be scared to make friends with people in your neighborhood. If you encounter problems, you and your friends can always fix them with teamwork. Then, you can laugh about it later!

POSITIVE FRIENDSHIP THOUGHTS

Timeless Friendship

Anaya Potts

Anaya and London have been friends ever since they met in the Lifetime Gym kids center. It was the day before the daddy/daughter dance. They were five and six years old. Today, they've been friends for more than ten years.

One day, Anaya headed over to London's house to hang out and talk. Anaya was excited as ever, but God had other plans when she got there. Anaya rang London's doorbell, excited for a full day of fun since it was summertime. Except, when London opened the door, she didn't look happy. Anaya wondered if something had happened, but she just brushed it off. She hoped that London would be happier once they started to play. Anaya waved goodbye to her mom as she drove off.

When Anaya and London got inside, Anaya said, "Hi, Maggie!" Maggie was the cutest dog ever.

London asked, "Anaya, do you want to watch TV?"

"Sure," Anaya said.

As they watched TV and talked, Anaya realized that London was quieter than usual. It seemed like she had something on her mind. Anaya decided to break the silence.

"London, are you okay?"

"I have to tell you something," London said as she led Anaya to her outside porch. "I have something big to tell you."

Anaya was very curious and excited. She couldn't wait to hear the news.

But nothing could have prepared her for what London was about to say.

"I'm moving to Pennsylvania," she said.

As soon as Anaya heard those words, her jaws dropped in shock. She felt like her world was collapsing on top of her. It hit her heart that her best friend was actually moving. This wasn't a joke, like they would usually play on each other. Anaya didn't know how to feel, but she tried to be happy for London.

As the next few weeks passed, Anaya watched London's house fill up with more boxes each time she visited. Anaya tried to stay happy and cherish the time that she had left with London, but it was growing harder by the day. Her best friend was leaving her, and she didn't know the next time she would see her.

Finally, the dreadful day came when Anaya had to say goodbye to London. As Anaya drove over to London's house, she tried to keep a smile on her face. However, inside, her heart was hurting. When she got there, she could tell London was feeling down, too. However, both of them tried to smile past the pain. Once the rest of the boxes were packed up into London's mom's car, it was time to say their final goodbyes. Anaya and London looked at each other for the last time and embraced for one final hug. They held each other tightly. They were scared to let go because they wouldn't see each other again for God knows how long. They stayed like that for minutes, which, at the time, felt too short.

Anaya's mom said, "It's time to go, Anaya," but she didn't want to leave. Anaya reluctantly let go of London slowly.

"I'm gonna miss you so much!" Anaya said. "You're my best friend and no one can replace you."

When Anaya got into her mom's car, she instantly felt a wave of sadness hit her. She wanted to cry, but she knew she couldn't cry at London's house. She tried her best to hold it in, but some tears managed to slip out. While Anaya looked at London's car from her car's back window, she wondered how London felt. She wondered if she was also crying. Maybe London felt the same pain. Anaya wondered if London would remember her. She wondered if they would talk often. She cried even more as she wondered who she would hang out with every weekend. Who would be her friend for all the activities they used to do together?

Anaya saw London's mom and her mom saying goodbye, as well. London's mom got into her car and started it. Anaya watched as London looked back one last time before her car sped off into the distance. On the ride home, Anaya stared out the window in sadness. She cried her eyes out that night because she missed her best friend already.

Over the next year, Anaya finally got her own cell phone. The first thing she did was contact London. Anaya was extremely excited because now she could FaceTime London and see her as they talked.

When London picked up the phone, Anaya felt a million years of joy rush into her heart. She and London spent the rest of the day talking. They spent the rest of the school year calling each other over FaceTime. They talked about their days, drama, school, and anything else that was on their minds. As the school year drew to an end, London and Anaya wished they could spend the whole summer together, like they used to when London lived in Michigan. However, it was highly unlikely since London lived so far away.

One day, London called Anaya urgently to tell her some good news.

"Guess what? I'm coming back to Michigan when school is out!"

As soon as Anaya heard the news, she jumped with joy. They started planning what they would do together since London would only be in Michigan for two weeks. When London arrived in Michigan, Anaya invited her over to her house immediately. They went swimming and ate tons of delicious food while they talked and laughed. It was truly the best day ever when they were reunited. They spent those two weeks doing fun activities, like bike riding, going to the movies, swimming, and simply giggling about life.

When it was almost time for London to go back to Pennsylvania, both of the girls were sad. The girls begged their parents to let London either stay in Michigan with Anaya for the rest of the summer, or let Anaya go with London to Pennsylvania for the rest of the summer. It took a lot of begging and pleading, but London's mom finally agreed to let Anaya go back with them for the remaining part of the summer. Anaya and London were filled with tears of joy. They were ready to have the best summer of their lives.

Anaya got dropped off at London's aunt's house on the day they were scheduled to leave. When London and Anaya saw each other, they were so excited for the ten-hour-long road trip ahead of them. They had games, movies and snacks. As they got on the road, they talked for hours. Anaya almost ate a whole bag of chips, while London fell asleep. When the girls woke up, they realized they were in the mountains when she looked out the window. They were so beautiful that Anaya took pictures with her phone.

After many breaks and stops, they finally made it to London's house. It was so cute, even in the dark. London and Anaya went up to London's room and crashed on her bed. They were knocked out as soon as their heads hit the pillows. They woke up the next morning, fully energized and ready for the full summer. However, on the first day back, London had to get a new physical for school because she had volleyball practice. Anaya would tag along and just watch her at practices. That whole summer, London and Anaya had a blast. They went on numerous road trips to different states. They went to many cool places, like Hershey's Chocolate World, where they ate many chocolates. They also visited a really cool humongous cave, which they got to walk inside and explore. Inside, they saw many beautiful crystals. They also bought cool souvenirs from the cave. In addition, they went to an outdoor course and bungee jumping in the mall, where they bought lots of souvenirs. They went to amusement parks and rode all the big rides. They stayed up late every night, eating delicious snacks and talking as they binge watched TV shows and browsed TikTok.

They walked to different restaurants and stores and even went swimming in London's pool every day. Many days, they would simply lay out under the sky, whether it was day or night. By the end of the summer, London and Anaya were inseparable again. However, Anaya still had to go back home. The road trip was a calm and quiet one. When they finally got to Anaya's house, and London and Anaya had to say goodbye, it wasn't a sad time. They were happy and full of joy. They had great hope. They knew that, one day soon, they would see each other again.

As the years progressed, COVID-19 shut the world down. During that time, London and Anaya connected on FaceTime daily. They ate on FaceTime. They did their homework on FaceTime. However, they couldn't physically see each other even if they wanted to because of the pandemic rules. Even when London came to Michigan, they had to stay away from each other. London's mom had just had a new baby and Anaya didn't want to get the baby sick. No matter what, though, they always stayed connected.

Two years later, London told Anaya on FaceTime that she would be moving back to Michigan! Anaya was beyond excited. She would finally have her best friend close to her again. When London got back to Michigan, the girls had an official sleepover, just like old times. London and Anaya hung out almost every day once London moved back, and they are still best friends today. Even though they were miles apart at times, they were inseparable. Through it all, they remained best friends and they would be forever. Nothing could ever change that.

POSITIVE FRIENDSHIP THOUGHTS

About So It Is Written

We help entrepreneurs write the ONE book that will expand their reach and get them to SIX figures in record time!

As the leading content curators for authorpreneurs and entrepreneurs, So It Is Written is best known for helping them package and leverage their expertise into a bestselling book, which amplifies their brand, accelerates their paydays and attracts bigger opportunities!

Let us help you brand in excellence as an author and entrepreneur so you can develop multiple streams of income from just ONE book!

Call us at 313-777-8607 today or email info@soitiswritten.net for more details about our services. We look forward to collaborating with you to make your project one of excellence!